Killer Cupcakes

Leighann Dobbs

Table of Contents

Other Works By Leighann Dobbs

Contemporary
Romance
* * *

Reluctant Romance
Forbidden Desires
Physical Attraction
Passionate Vengeance
Second Chances

Lexy Baker
Cozy Mystery Series
* * *

Killer Cupcakes
Dying For Danish
Murder, Money, & Marzipan
3 Bodies and a Biscotti

Blackmoore Sisters Romantic
Cozy Mystery Series
* * *

Dead Wrong

Dobbs "Fancytales"
Regency Romance Fairytales Series
* * *

Something In Red
Snow White and the Seven Rogues

This is a work of fiction. None of it is real.

All names, places, and events are products of the author's imagination. Any resemblance to real names, places, or events are purely coincidental, and should not be construed as being real.

10 9 8 7 6 5 4 3 2 1

Cover by http://www.coverkicks.com

***

This book is dedicated to my husband, Bruce. Thanks for always believing in me and supporting my dreams. I love you more than words can say.

***

Chapter One

"Sprinkles - no!" Lexy hissed at her dog who was wriggling through the gap in the backyard fence.

With a sigh of resignation, she padded out into the yard in her bare feet, her pink cotton pajama bottoms fluttering around her calves in the late night, summer breeze. The glow of the full moon lit the yard well enough for Lexy to see where she was going without a flashlight.

She reached the gap in the fence and turned sideways to squeeze through. Despite her slim size, she had to push to make it. Rip!

Lexy looked down. Her favorite pajama bottoms - the ones speckled with cute images of fluffy cherry-topped cupcakes - now had a gigantic rip in the side. Perfect.

She felt an uncustomary flare of irritation at her dog. Was it too much to ask for the dog to simply run out in the yard, do her business, and run back in?

Lexy had images of running through the neighborhood in the dark, her ripped pajamas flapping behind her, frantically chasing her dog while neighbors peered through their windows at the crazy lady. It wasn't the way she had imagined meeting her new neighbors. Luckily most of them were elderly and, since it was 10:00 at night, hopefully they were all in bed.

She cleared the fence and emerged in the neighbors backyard just in time to see Sprinkles squatting in an impeccably groomed flower garden.

"No!" She hissed again, but the dog was determined.

Rushing over, Lexy grabbed Sprinkles by the collar and gave a silent thanks she had remembered to bring a poop bag. Whipping it from her pocket, she knelt down to scoop Sprinkles's little gift into the bag, the sharp corners of the bark mulch poking into her bare feet.

A slight movement to her right sent a jolt of panic through her heart. Still squatting down, she turned her head and her eyes fell on a pair of thick, heavy, black boots. Men's boots.

Lexy slowly scanned her eyes upwards. Slightly faded jeans. Slim waist. Broad chest covered by an, almost too small, black tee shirt. Was this one of her elderly neighbors?

Her eyes completed their upwards journey and stopped at a ruggedly handsome face. Slightly tanned with honey brown eyes and framed with dark, close cut hair. Nope, definitely not elderly.

Mr. Ruggedly Handsome, whoever he was, stared down at her with a smirk on his face. Suddenly, Lexy felt like a child who had been caught doing something naughty.

"Can I help you?" His voice sounded a bit gruff with a hint of annoyance.

Lexy felt her cheeks grow hot with embarrassment. Straightening her shoulders, she made an effort to stand and try to retain some dignity, or at least as much dignity as one could while squatting in cupcake pajamas to scoop a pile of poop.

She felt the bark mulch shifting under her feet, struggling to gain control, Lexy fell backwards her arms flapping at her sides like a bird trying to take flight. Mr. Handsome shot out an arm to steady her, but not before she crashed into the side of a large rhododendron, breaking off one of it's branches. Lexy felt her cheeks burn even hotter.

"Oh gosh, I'm so sorry," she sputtered, putting her index finger up to her eye to stop the annoying nervous twitch that was starting in her lower lid. "My dog got out of my yard through the fence." She pointed towards the edge of the back yard where the gap in the fence abutted the edge of her back yard.

She shoved her hand out towards the man. "I'm Lexy Baker."

His eyebrows shot up. "You're Mona's granddaughter?"

She nodded, taking his hand. It was warm, and the handshake was firm. Lexy felt an alarming tingle as they shook hands.

"I'm Jack Perillo. This is my house." He gestured with his free hand to indicate the house they were standing next to.

“How is Mona?” His forehead creased in a frown and he looked her up and down as if trying to decide if she was a suitable replacement for his backyard neighbor.

“Oh, she’s fine - she loves it over at the Senior housing complex.” Lexy felt a wave of uncustomary self consciousness under Jack’s scrutiny. She looked down at her torn pajamas and realized she must look a sight in her bare feet, ripped pajamas and no makeup. Who could blame him for looking at her like she was some sort of deranged criminal.

She noticed Sprinkles had made her way over to Jack and was enthusiastically sniffing his shoes.

“This is my dog, Sprinkles,” she said pointing at the small dog.

“Sprinkles?” Jack snorted out a laugh, his right eyebrow raised up in a question. Lexy couldn’t tell if the laugh was in good humor or he was mocking her, but she felt her heart melting when he bent down to stroke the fur of the little white dog.

“Hi Sprinkles, I hope you don’t keep using my garden for your bathroom because I.....” Jack was interrupted by the sound of a doorbell coming from his pants pocket. He straightened up and pulled a cell phone out.

"Perillo." He barked into the phone, he listened for a few seconds the creases on his forehead growing deeper. "I'll be right there."

Jack snapped the phone shut and nodded towards Lexy. "Sorry, but business calls." He held up the phone. "Nice to meet you Ms. Baker."

Turning abruptly, he set off in the direction of the driveway. "And don't forget to pick up that mess, it's not good for the plants." He shot over his shoulder, walking away and leaving Lexy to wonder if she just made a friend or an enemy.

***

Jack turned the corner of his house and couldn't help the grin forming on his face. His new neighbor was kind of cute, he thought.

He chuckled to himself, remembering how her grandmother, Mona, would always sneak in a mention of her with a certain twinkle in her eye -

Jack knew Mona had visions of fixing them up, but he always changed the subject because he didn't have time for any women in his life, right now.

But tonight Jack had felt something stir inside him which he hadn't felt in a long time...something which might cause him to break his vow of bachelorhood. He hoped he hadn't been too harsh with her about the dog poop. Maybe he would have to make an excuse to drop in on her some night. He wouldn't mind seeing Lexy Baker again, thats for sure.

Little did he know, it would be less than 24 hours before he saw her again and the circumstances wouldn't be as pleasant as he was hoping.

Chapter Two

Lexy woke the next morning to a beautiful summer day. She rolled over on her back and felt the comforting warmth of the small body next to her. She reached under the covers to pet the silky fur.

With a wistful sigh, Lexy realized Sprinkles had been the only warm body in her bed since her breakup with Kevin two years earlier.

Thoughts of warm bodies in her bed, reminded her of Jack, the neighbor she had met the previous night. Lexy had felt attracted to him despite his gruff demeanor. She wondered if she would see him again. *Did she even want to?*

Lexy pushed thoughts of Jack out of her mind. After what she had been through with Kevin, she wasn't sure she was ready to trust anyone again and, besides, she had her new bakery to run and no time for romance.

Thinking of her bakery, the *Cup and Cake,* brought a smile to her face. Lexy had loved baking, even as a little girl and had always dreamt of having her own bakery. After selling their house to travel the country in an RV earlier in the year, her parents had helped her make her dream come true by lending her the money to open the bakery.

She'd chosen a small storefront in an old mill building located in downtown Brook Ridge Falls. Her bakery and small cafe had done very well. Lexy was focused on the success of the her new business and that, along with Sprinkles, were about all she had time for.

Sprinkles poked her face out from under the covers, putting her chin on Lexy's chest and staring at her intently as if willing Lexy to get up and fill her food bowl.

"OK, my friend, let's get up and get going." Lexy pulled back the covers and Sprinkles bounded out of the bed, ready to start the day. Lexy swung her legs over the side, hopped out of bed with almost as much energy as Sprinkles and made her way to the closet.

She pulled out a pair of jeans and a pink tee-shirt. Dressing for work was easy since jeans and tee-shirts were her unofficial uniform. She had a variety of vintage aprons she wore to give her bakery a nostalgic appeal and protect her clothes from flour and frosting, so she didn't fuss too much about what she wore underneath.

What she wore on her feet, however, were another matter. Lexy had an obsession with shoes - the higher the heels and the more expensive the better. Her closet was a shoe lovers paradise with custom racks and bins that would turn any fashionista green with envy.

Lexy bit the inside of her cheek trying to decide which pair to wear. Her eyes scanned the rows, arraigned by color until they fell on a cute pink number by Steve Madden. They were stilettos with a platform toe, ankle straps and stainless steel studs.

She pulled them from their slot and brought them over to the bed. Sitting, she slipped them on her feet, feeling the soft texture of the suede under her fingertips. She stood and marveled at how the shoes brought her from a short five foot one to a respectable five foot four. Sure, her feet might hurt after standing on them all day, but Lexy loved the extra height and was used to wearing tall stilettos and platforms. Standing sideways in front of the mirror she admired the shoes from all angles. *Perfect!*

Glancing at her watch, Lexy cursed under her breath. She had only 15 minutes to finish getting ready and make the short drive to the bakery!

She quickly pulled her medium length mink colored hair into a pony tail and dabbed on some lip gloss. A light brush of mascara made her green eyes stand out against her tanned skin.

Racing down the stairs, she heard the grandmother clock in the dining room chime the quarter hour. She rushed through the cozy living room to the kitchen, pausing only a second to feel grateful for her good fortune to be living there.

The house had been her grandmothers but Mona, or Nans as Lexy called her, had decided a few months earlier she would have more fun if she moved into the *Brook Ridge Retirement Community* - the senior housing where all her friends were. She had asked Lexy to move in and take care of the house and Lexy had happily agreed. With limited space in senior housing, Mona had left most of the furniture and the home still had a magical feeling of comfort and safety Lexy remembered from her childhood.

Reaching the kitchen at high speed, Lexy scooped up Sprinkle's pink dog bowl and filled it with dog food from a stainless steel canister she kept handy on the counter. Glancing out the window, she couldn't help but sneak a peek through the gap in the fence at Jack's house. *Was he home?*

Sprinkles danced in circles waiting for her food bowl, her nails making clicking noises which stole Lexy's attention from the window. She bent down, placing the bowl in front of the dog.

"You be a good girl." She scratched the little dog behind the ears, then hearing her own stomach growl, she stepped over to the fridge.

Pulling the door open, she reached in and grabbed an eclair. Giving silent thanks that she was blessed with a high metabolism, Lexy shoved the end of it in her mouth. The cold, creamy filling coated her taste buds and she heard herself making little "nummy" sounds.

She stood there for a moment enjoying the rest of the eclair, then rummaged in the fridge for something to eat on the way in to work. She felt lucky she could eat whatever she wanted without gaining an ounce because it allowed her to bring home all the day-old bakery items she didn't want to sell in the store and enjoy them herself.

Grabbing a cream cheese frosted pumpkin muffin, she closed the fridge door, then grabbing her keys from the key rack, she ran out the side door to her car.

***

Lexy rushed through the backdoor of the *Cup and Cake* without a minute to spare. She took a deep breath, the aroma of sugary baked goodness filling her nose. She stood there a moment to savor it.

"Morning!" Her perpetually cheerful assistant Cassie, appeared in the kitchen doorway. Her magenta hair spiked up on her head gave the impression of an exotic bird. The vintage 1940s cherry patterned apron she wore was already covered with something red and gooey.

"You're in early today," Lexy said with a smile. Best friends since high school, Cassie always made Lexy smile. She had hired her when she opened the bakery and Cassie had proven to be an invaluable asset with her artistic creativity and dedication to the success of the bakery.

Lexy kept a peg rack by the door with a selection of vintage aprons. She choose a light green one with big pink cabbage roses on the front. Slipping it over her head, she peeked out into the main bakery area.

"Is anyone here yet?" The front of the store had a large window with an amazing view of the waterfall. To take advantage of this, Lexy had recently setup a few tables in front of it so people could eat their pastries and have tea or coffee while enjoying the view.

"No." Cassie checked her watch. "I was just about to open, though."

Lexy nodded, she could smell the pungent aroma of coffee brewing. “Thanks for starting the coffee, what do you have going in back?”

“This morning, I’m doing some raspberry turnovers.” Cassie said, pointing down to the red gooey stuff on her apron.

Cassie usually liked to get in before the bakery opened for customers so she could concentrate on some baking without interruption. Then, once open, the girls took turns at watching the front and baking in back. Their long time friendship kept them in tune and enabled them to synchronize the day perfectly. The arrangement worked for them both.

“OK, you keep at it and I’ll open up and then tidy some of the cases and put some of the freshly baked goods out.” Lexy pointed her chin towards the large glass front cases where the baked goods were displayed.

Cassie nodded and turned back to the kitchen. Lexy made her way to the front door. Unlocking it and turning the sign on the door to Open.

Grabbing some paper towels and a spray bottle filled with organic cleaner, she opened the big case in the middle of the store and started removing some of the items inside. She brought out trays of cannoli's, eclairs's, half moons and some of her signature pieces - cupcake tops, and placed them on top of the case.

Wriggling to get a good position for cleaning, Lexy had her front half in the case, her back end sticking up in the air when the tinkle of the bells over the door alerted her to the presence of a customer.

"Just a sec." She said, extracting herself from the case like a contortionist climbing out of a trunk.

"How can I help yo....." Her words were cut off, her mouth forming a surprised O when recognition dawned on her. Standing on the other side of the case was Jack Perillo, her neighbor. But somehow he looked different. It took her a minute to realize the difference was the official looking badge he was holding in front of her face.

"Oh... Hi." She said, her mind whirling. *Did he come just to visit her? And what was the badge all about?*

"Hi Lexy." Lexy saw a look of discomfort pass his face. He quickly added, "I'm a detective with the BRPD, and, unfortunately, I need to ask you some questions."

"Questions?" Lexy felt her face eyebrows knit together in confusion. "I don't understand. What's this about? Did something happen to my grandmother?"

"No, Mona is fine, it's about your boyfriend Kevin."

"Kevin? He's my *ex* boyfriend. I haven't seen him in almost two years."

"Well, I'm sorry to tell you he was found dead. Murdered."

The impact of the news hit Lexy like a ton of bricks. *Murdered? Kevin?* Even though they had broken up two years ago, *and* he had treated her badly, she still felt a pang of sympathy for him.

“Murdered? But what does that have to do with *me*?”

“Well, that’s the thing,” Jack said, his face a mask of stone. “He was found face down in a box of your cupcake tops...they were poisoned.”

Lexy felt a jolt of shock, her head was swimming, her ankles starting to feel wobbly. She grabbed the side of the display case to steady herself, wishing that, just for once, she had the good sense to wear shoes with a lower heel.

Chapter Three

Jack put his hand on Lexy's arm to steady her. He couldn't help but think how pretty she looked. Vulnerable. Last night he had thought she was cute in her pajamas, but today with makeup on he realized she was a knock out.

"Maybe we should go sit over at the tables." He pointed his chin towards the cafe tables setup by the window. Without waiting for an answer, he put an arm around Lexy guiding her towards them. *No wonder she's wobbly, look at those crazy shoes she has on.*

Jack remembered the distinct imprint of stiletto heels outside Kevin's front door. *Coincidence?* Lots of women wore stilettos. Lots of women probably visited Kevin, but still, Jack made a note in his head that Lexy *was* wearing them herself.

Jack seated Lexy at a table, pulling out the chair on the opposite side, he carefully settled his 5 foot 11 frame in the delicate wrought iron seat.

"I'm sorry, but I have to ask you a few questions."

"OK." Lexy seemed to be recovering from the initial shock. Jack thought he saw a hint of suspicion cross her face. He also noticed her right lower eye lid was twitching. *Just nerves or a sign of guilt?*

Jack pulled a well worn notebook from his jacket pocket. Flipping open the black leather cover, he turned to an empty page. Producing a pencil from his other pocket, he sat poised to write.

"Where were you last night?"

Lexy paused a moment, then "I was in your garden picking up dog poop."

Jack felt a smile cross his face. "Yes, true ... but before that?"

"Well, I worked until 7:00 p.m. here at the bakery. Then went home, ate supper, watched some T.V. then got ready for bed and took the dog out." She leaned towards him in her chair. Jack saw her green eyes narrow. "Wait a minute, you don't think *I* did it, do you?"

Jack could see she was starting to get angry, so he used his best soothing voice. "We have to ask these questions to rule you out...of course I don't think you did it." *He didn't, did he?*

Lexy settled back in her chair pacified by Jack's words. He continued the line of questioning.

"Did anyone see you here, or at home last night?"

Lexy bit her lower lip. "My assistant Cassie saw me here until 5:00, then she left. After that I was alone until I saw you at about 9:30 in the backyard."

Jack nodded jotting the timeframes down in his book. "When did you last see Kevin?"

"Well, it will be two years in October. We had a nasty breakup. I haven't seen him since."

"A nasty breakup?" Jack felt his forehead wrinkle in concern. For a moment he wondered if she still held a grudge...one deep enough to make her turn to murder. "Tell me about the breakup, was it violent?"

Lexy squirmed in her chair. The look on her face made it evident she didn't like talking about her breakup.

"We did argue a lot towards the end. He cheated on me. Lied to me. We didn't part friends, but it wasn't physically violent or anything." Lexy was glancing down at the floor, her cheeks a slight shade of red as she recalled the breakup.

Jack might normally have continued to probe for more information but he was already developing a soft spot for Lexy so he cut the interview short...but not before he had to deliver one more piece of bad news.

***

Across the table, Jack gently closed his notebook. Lexy got the feeling she wasn't going to like what he had to say next.

"I'm sorry, I have a warrant here granting us access to your kitchen. We'll have to test all your baked goods and ingredients." He pulled a document out of his jacket and put it on the table. "You'll have to close the bakery so we can get the job done."

Lexy felt the air rush out of her lungs. *Close the bakery?* The bakery was her bread and butter, she would be losing money every day it was closed. With things as tight as they were she could ill afford it.

"What" For how long?" She sputtered, the sting of tears pricking her eyes. *She was being treated like a criminal when she hadn't even done anything wrong!*

Jack reached across the table resting his hand over hers. "I'll push to get it done as quickly as possible. I promise."

He released her hand, standing up from the table. Through the window, Lexy saw a big blue van pull into the alley leading to the back of the bakery. "There's the lab van now, you can stay to watch or you can leave, but I'll have to ask you not to touch anything or get in the way if you stay."

Lexy stared up at him. She couldn't believe this was happening. She felt her anger growing like a quick rising bread dough.

"Uhhh... What's going on?" Cassie appeared in the entrance to the front room. Lexy turned to her, her anger softening a few notches at the look of concern on her friends face.

"Cassie, This is Detective Jack Perillo." Lexy waved her hand towards Jack. "It seems someone poisoned Kevin with a box of our cupcake tops and now we have to close down the bakery so they can investigate."

Cassie crossed the bakery to Lexy and Jack, her boots making hollow sounds on the tile floor.

"Who would do that?" Her head swiveled from Lexy to Jack. "Surely you don't think *we* had anything to do with it?" She stared at Jack, her face a mask of angry disgust.

Jack took a step back. "No ma'am," he said. "But we have to do our due diligence. We'll have you back in business in no time."

Cassie looked at him sideways. From the disdain on her face it was clear she didn't believe him. Lexy felt alarm as she saw Cassie's face getting redder.

"Cassie, it's OK." She stood giving her friend a hug in an attempt to diffuse any angry confrontation between Cassie and the detective. "I think maybe it would be best if we left them to do their work here. I'll come back later to make sure everything is in order."

Lexy glanced over at Jack. "What time will you be done?"

"It's hard to say, maybe I should give you a call when we are finishing up?" Jack took out his phone, ready to plug Lexy's number in.

Lexy rattled off her cell phone number reluctantly. Earlier in the day she might have been happy to give Jack Perillo her phone number, but right now she was feeling quite a bit of anger towards the detective, even if he was pretty good looking.

Jack took a card from his top pocket holding it out towards Lexy. "Here's my number. I'd appreciate a call if you think of anything relevant to the case."

Lexy grabbed onto the card by the edge so as to avoid brushing her fingers against his. She slid it into her back pocket. "I guess you should let your people in now," she said curtly, nodding towards the back of the bakery, "I'll show you to the door."

She turned around heading towards the back with Cassie and Jack in tow.

In the back, Lexy and Cassie waited for the herd of police personnel to stream by before taking off their aprons and hanging them up on the pegs.

Lexy poked her head into the kitchen area. "The ovens are on, I guess you will have to turn them off since I can't touch anything," she said to no one in particular. Turning on her heel, she rushed out the door. With her pony tail swishing from the momentum, she brushing past Jack without even a glance.

Lexy felt Jack's eyes boring into her back as she walked away. *Did he think she did it?*

Even though he had assured her he didn't think she was the murderer, Lexy got the distinct feeling she might be at the top of the detectives suspect list.

Chapter Four

In the parking lot, Cassie stopped short whirling around to face Lexy. "I can't believe they can just do this!" she sputtered, her face screwed up in anger. "They'll probably misplace everything ... my turnovers will be ruined!"

Lexy patted Cassie on the back, forcing herself to be calm. She knew Cassie had a short fuse, once she got going, anything could happen. The last thing she needed now was to be bailing Cassie out of jail for obstructing a police investigation.

"It's OK, Cass," she soothed. "They're just doing their jobs. When they don't find anything suspicious we can reopen and go on as usual."

"But, who would do this?" Cassie voiced the question Lexy had been thinking.

"I have no idea. Kevin was kind of a jerk, but I don't think he was bad enough for someone to want to *kill* him." Lexy tapped her fingernail on her bottom teeth, her forehead wrinkled in thought. "... And, why do it with our cupcake tops?"

The cupcake tops were Lexy's signature pastry. Since she was a kid, Lexy had always eaten only the frosted tops of cupcakes because that was the most tasty part. The bottoms seemed dry in comparison, so she just nibbled off the tops tossing the bottoms out or using them in other dessert dishes.

Lexy thought others might feel the same way about cupcakes, so she started selling just the tops loaded with frosting and packaged in special cupcake holders and boxes. They were a huge hit and a big part of what had made her so successful. She felt a pang of panic in her chest. Hopefully this whole incident wouldn't hurt sales.

Cassie shuffled her feet, a look of indecision on her face. "I'm not sure what to do now."

"Me either," Lexy shrugged. "I guess we'll just let them do their job. I'll call you when they are done. We can meet back here to lock up and straighten everything out, if you want."

"Yes, I want to help you any way I can." The genuine concern in her friends eyes warmed Lexy's heart.

"Don't worry, Cassie, everything will work out. It *has* to. I don't know who did this or why, but I do know one thing," glancing back at the bakery, Lexy's mouth formed a hard line, "I'm not going to sit back and leave it up to the BRPD to figure this out. We need to get back up and running right away or it could be very bad for business."

***

Lexy sat in her yellow VW bug in the parking lot contemplating her next move. She was deep in thought, when her cell phone broke the silence.

Digging it out of her purse, she flipped it open. "Hello?"

"Lexy, *Dear!*" Her mother's exuberant greeting burst from the phone, her voice about twenty decibels louder than necessary. Lexy held the phone out six inches from her ear.

"Hi Mom, how are you?" Lexy's parents had left earlier in the year on a tour of the United States in an RV. They were visiting all kinds of tourist attractions and relatives while having the time of their lives. Her parents were still happily in love after 34 years of marriage. Lexy let out a small sigh, wondering if she would ever be lucky enough to have the same kind of relationship.

"Oh, we're doing wonderful dear! Your father made the most delicious potato dish over the campfire last night. We're just starting out this morning to Cawker City, Kansas to see the worlds largest ball of twine."

"The worlds largest ball of twine?" Lexy felt her eyebrows lifting up in question. She didn't even know there was such a thing, never mind that people would travel to see it. But, if there was some oddball attraction to be seen, it would be just like her mother to want to go there.

"Oh yes, it's 1.6 million feet of twine and weighs almost 18,000 pounds!"

"Wow, that sounds...ummm...big." Lexy said the most polite thing she could think of given her mothers obvious excitement about the large collection of string.

"I just called to see how you are doing, dear." Her mother called to check on her a couple of times a week, to update her on their travels and make sure Lexy was OK. Lexy usually looked forward to the calls, but today she had other things on her mind.

"Oh, I'm fine Mom, glad you and Dad are doing well and having fun. I'm a little busy right at the moment, though can I call you later?" Lexy had no intention of telling her mother about Kevin's murder. She didn't want to spoil their fun or make them worry.

"Of course, but I did want to ask you to check in on Nans if you can, we worry about her all alone over at the retirement community."

A light bulb went off in Lexy's head. *Of course, Nans would be able to help!* Lexy had gone to Nans with all her problems since she was a small child somehow her grandmother could always make things better, no matter what the problem.

"Sure, Mom. I'll go visit her today."

"Great! Well, I'll let you go, Dad and I both love you!"

"Me too, Mom." Lexy snapped the phone shut. Putting her car in gear, she backed out of her parking spot, heading towards the exit in the front of the building.

She winced as she saw several policemen standing in front of the bakery, one of them being Jack. He looked over at her as she drove by, raising a hand in a friendly wave. Lexy plastered a smile on her face and waved back. She felt like giving him the finger, but she figured it might be smarter to stay on his good side. Having a friend in the police department might prove to be very helpful if she wanted things to go her way.

Chapter Five

The lobby at the Brook Ridge Retirement Community center was comfortably furnished with overstuffed sofas and several tables and chairs. On most days, Nans could usually be found here socializing with other residents. Lexy was accustomed to just popping in to visit without the need to call first.

Lexy surveyed the lobby for her grandmother. Her eyes scanned past two men playing chess at a table near the window to a trio of elderly women parked on the sofa watching a talk show on TV, finally coming to rest on Nans and three older women sitting at a round table their hands moving excitedly as they talked.

Nans looked up, spotting her in the doorway, a huge smile appearing on her face. “Lexy!” Despite her current problems, Lexy couldn’t help but smile at the site of her perky 5 foot 1 grandmother leaping up from the table and rushing over to greet her.

“Hi Nans!” The older woman enveloped Lexy in a big hug causing a comforting warmth to soothe Lexy’s troubled heart.

“I didn’t know you were coming today, dear,” Nans said. “I would have made some tea-”

Lexy interrupted, “Oh, no worries Nans - I was in the neighborhood and ... well... I have a little problem I’d like to talk to you about.”

Nans eyes grew large. “Oh, well then come over here, dear.” She took Lexy’s hand, leading her to a secluded area of the lobby which had two large wingback chairs set at an angle facing each other. Nans plopped down in one, motioning for Lexy to sit in the other.

Nans leaned forward in her chair. “Now, tell me, what is the problem? ... Why are you winking”

“It’s just a nervous eye twitch Nans...its been happening for a while now just when I get nervous or tired.”

“Oh well, try putting some cucumber slices on them, that should help,” Nans said. “Was that the problem you wanted to talk to me about?”

"No, Nans. This is something much more serious...."

Lexy told Nans about Kevin - how he had been poisoned, allegedly, with her cupcake tops and how her bakery had been shut down until the police could investigate.

Nans patted her knee. "Now, now dear. Don't you worry. This sounds like a perfect case for the Ladies Detective Club. I'm sure we can have it solved for you in no time!"

"The Ladies Detective Club?" Lexy felt her forehead wrinkle, "What's *that*?"

"Oh, it's a little club the ladies and I have put together." Nans nodded over at the women around the table where she had been sitting when Lexy arrived. "We've become quite good at solving murders and mysteries."

"You solve murders?" Lexy said feeling her eyes grow wide.

"Yes, dear. Well, not officially. We do it behind the scenes, so to speak. We follow the coverage of the crimes, put the clues together and figure out who the perpetrator is." Nans beamed with obvious pride.

"I had no idea...."

"Well, we ladies have to have something to occupy our time with," Nans said with a conspiratorial wink. "Come on over, I'll introduce you to the girls."

Nans led Lexy over to the table. "Ladies, this is my granddaughter, Lexy. Lexy, this is Ida, Helen and Ruth." Nans pointed to each lady who nodded their heads in turn.

Nans pulled a chair over from a neighboring table pointing at it for Lexy to sit. Nans sat in her own seat. Getting straight to the point, she said, "Lexy has a murder for us to solve."

Ida, Ruth and Helen's faces perked up. "Oh do tell," Ida said, excitement gleaming in her eyes.

Lexy recounted the story with Nans interjecting every so often to give her opinion. When she was done, the women all expressed their dismay at her situation.

"Well, I think we can help find who did this, don't you agree?" Nans asked the other three ladies. Three grayish blue heads nodded in unison.

"Great!" Nans clapped her hands together. The first thing is to get on the internet and Google Kevin, see if we can find out what he was up to which might have gotten him murdered," Nans said.

Lexy stared at her. "You use the internet?"

"Of course, we do silly.... We use these..." Nans bent over, rummaging in her giant old lady purse which she seemed to always have with her. She pulled out a shiny new iPad causing Lexy's eyes to widen in astonishment.

As if on cue, Ida, Ruth and Helen all bent down fishing in their giant old lady purses each pulling out their own iPad.

"You see," Nans said, "we follow the case online and on TV. We can find out all the clues and solve the crime without even leaving the complex! Of course, we *can* leave if we need to do some field work because Ruth still drives so we can go in her car."

Lexy felt her mouth fall open, her mind conjuring up images of four old ladies in trench coats descending on the streets of Brook Ridge interrogating witnesses and hunting for clues.

"Oh, *and* we have an *in* with the police department," Nans said out of the corner of her mouth. "My old neighbor, Jack Perillo, is a detective there. You might want to look him up, his backyard abuts the backyard of my house ... well *your* house now. He could help get you cleared." Nans shot Lexy a sly look.

"Oh, we've met," Lexy said with a sigh, "he's in charge of the murder case actually."

"Such a nice young man..." Nans let her words trail off a far away look in her eye.

Lexy didn't want to delve into the thoughts Nans might be having, so she brought everyone's attention back to the problem at hand. "So, what do you ladies suggest I do. I can't sit around waiting for the police to handle this, I need my bakery open right away!"

Ida spoke up next. “You need to go to the wake, of course. The murderer always shows up at the wake.”

The other ladies nodded in unison.

“Yes, that should be your first step. Look for anyone suspicious. Talk to everyone who knew Kevin. You need to look for the people who had means, motive and opportunity,” Nans advised.

Means, motive and opportunity? Lexy wondered when Nans had become so proficient in police jargon. Apparently living next to a police detective had it’s effect on ones vocabulary.

Sitting back in her seat, Nans looked Lexy in the eye, her lips set in a serious line. “Lexy, I think your bakery being closed is the least of your worries. It looks to me like someone is trying to frame you for Kevin’s murder.”

Lexy snorted out a short laugh. “Nans, I think you’ve been watching too much TV, why would someone want to frame me for murdering Kevin?”

Chapter Six

Sprinkles came running from the kitchen to greet Lexy the second she opened the door. Lexy bent down scooping her up in her arms allowing the dog to plant wet kisses on her face. The unconditional love of the little dog made her feel all warm and happy inside.

Lexy's momentary happiness was short lived. Remembering what Nans had said less than an hour ago at the senior center caused butterflies of uneasiness to take up residence in her stomach. Could it be true? *Was* someone trying to frame her? And, if so, why?

Lexy didn't have any enemies that she knew of. *Could it be someone who wants to harm her business. A competitor, maybe?*

She didn't know of any other bakeries in the area. She couldn't imagine who would go to such lengths just to ruin a business.

Her cellphone went off, sounding abnormally loud in the silence. Lexy jumped, her heart racing. She dove for it, hoping it was Jack announcing they could go back to the bakery. It was Cassie.

"Hi Cass, I haven't heard anything yet."

"Oh." Cassie's voice had a note of dejection. "I was thinking we could get together to brainstorm a suspect list."

Nans had said Lexy should start looking for people with means, motive and opportunity, but hearing Cassie suggest it too made the whole thing seem so overly dramatic. Then again, with the bakery closed they had nothing better to do so, why not?

"OK, come on over, we'll see what we can figure out while we wait for Jack to call," Lexy said.

"Right, be there in a jiff!"

Lexy hung up the phone. Growling sounds were coming from her stomach reminding her it had been hours since she had eaten. She headed towards the kitchen, Sprinkles following along happily at her heels. She went straight for the fridge. It was loaded with day old goodies from the bakery. Lexy looked at them feeling uncertainty roil in her gut. *Poison?*

She shook her head, she knew nothing was wrong with her baked goods. No one else had turned up dead because of eating them. Kevin's cupcakes were obviously tampered with *after* they were bought from her. Which meant the killer must have been in the bakery that day ... or sent someone to buy the cupcake tops.

Lexy made a mental note to try to remember all the customers who had bought cupcake tops in the days before Kevin's murder.

Hunger pangs forced her attention back to the bakery boxes stacked in her fridge. She picked out a box of cupcake tops and a gallon of milk. Reaching into the box, she grabbed two tops - both had chocolate cake with heavy chocolate frosting. *Just what a girl suspected of murdering her ex needs to make things better.*

Lexy unscrewed the top of the milk container, the cap slipped from her fingers clattering hollowly on the floor. Sprinkles was on it in a flash. Batting the top like a cat and chasing it around the room. It was an odd behavior for a dog but Sprinkles had done it since she was a puppy. Any small item which fell on the floor was fair game for her to play with. Lexy always joked that the small dog must be part cat.

Laughing, Lexy started after the little dog joining in the game of chase until she finally retrieved the top. Washing it off, she poured her glass, then put the milk back in the fridge. Grabbing her plate she sat at the table to enjoy her cupcake tops while she waited for Cassie.

***

Lexy closed her eyes and bit into the last morsel of decadently chocolate cupcake, focusing every fiber of her being on the sweet, smooth taste of the chocolate and blocking out any stressful or negative thoughts. *Tap Tap.* Peering over at the small window in the kitchen door where the noise was coming from, she saw a spray of shockingly pink hair. *Cassie.*

Lexy jumped up to let her in. Cassie was in her usual after work attire - black tee-shirt, black leather skirt and black boots which she wore year round. Lexy couldn't help but wonder how her feet didn't suffocate in the hot summer sun.

"Hi!" Cassie greeted her exuberantly, giving her a big hug which Lexy gladly returned.

"Come on in." Lexy stood aside to let Cassie enter. Pointing to one of the chairs at the table, she said, "Have a seat."

Lexy sat opposite her, telling her about her visit with Nans and how the Ladies Detective Club had suggested she go to the wake.

"That's a great idea!" Cassie agreed. "You might be able to connect with some of your old friends who were still friendly with Kevin. They might have some clues about what he was up to. I'd love to go with you, but I promised Brandon I'd take over his Tae Kwon Do class."

Brandon, Cassie's brother, owned a fitness studio downtown and Cassie often taught classes there. His wife had just had a baby and Lexy knew it was important for Cassie to be there for him to fill in.

"That's OK," she reassured her friend. "I feel a little awkward considering my history with Kevin...and umm...well the circumstances...but I would like to give my condolences to Jason."

Lexy felt a twinge of sympathy for Jason, Kevin's brother. The two had always had a rivalry of sorts with Kevin being the black sheep and Jason being able to do no wrong.

Where Kevin had a dead-end job on the docks, Jason had educated himself and risen to be the deputy mayor of their little town. Lexy had remained friends with Jason even through her nasty breakup with Kevin. Even now, years later, they still had lunch together every couple of months.

Lexy suspected Jason wanted to be more than friends, he'd hinted at it several times, but she always rebuked his advances because she wasn't interested. She did, however, value his friendship and knowing the deputy mayor did have its advantages - Jason had been a big help when she needed to secure permits to open the bakery.

"OK, lets try to come up with some people we can get in touch with who might have known what

Kevin was doing that could have gotten him killed." Lexy pulled a piece of paper and pen from a drawer and sat poised to write.

"He didn't hang around much with the old gang once he started working at the docks, but I know Tom McGraw worked there with him... I could probably talk to him. He's a friend of Brandon's," Cassie offered.

"Great! That's a good start." Lexy bit her lower lip, looking up at the ceiling trying to recall any friends of Kevin's who they might have in common. "What about Chuck and Sandy from the pub?"

Cassie nodded. Lexy added their names to the list.

The girls went back and forth suggesting names and writing them down for a good hour, until they were interrupted by Lexy's phone.

She ran into the living room grabbing it off the sofa table where she had left it earlier.

"Hello."

"Hi Lexy, it's Jack Perillo." She recognized the voice on the other end before he even said his name.

"Hi." Lexy held her breath, waiting for him to tell her the outcome of the investigation. Her stomach jittery with nerves.

The sounds of Jack nervously clearing his throat came through the phone. "Well, the good news is we're done at the bakery and you are free to go back in..."

"And what's the bad news?" She felt her voice rising in a panic. *Had they found something in the bakery?*

"There was too much for us to go through on-site so we had to take all your ingredients to the lab for testing ... I can't clear you to open for business until the testing is completed."

"What?" Lexy cried into the phone. She felt all her muscles tensing up as anger boiled through her. Lexy saw Cassie come around the corner from the kitchen, a questioning look on her face.

"I'm sorry Lexy," Jack said. "I'm trying to rush it along but we have to look at everything."

Lexy felt like someone had punched her in the gut. Not only could she *not* open the bakery, she would have to restock all the ingredients too. Deep down she knew none of this was Jack's fault, but her anger was directed at him anyway.

"OK. Thanks. I'll use my spare key...you can return mine later." She said abruptly into the phone, then snapped it shut without even a goodbye.

She turned to Cassie. "We can go back to the bakery, but we can't open for business yet. They've taken all our ingredients so we'll have to restock."

Lexy saw Cassie's lips purse, her eyes narrowing. She didn't want her friend going off on a tirade, so she tried to think on the bright side. She took a deep breath and released her tension and anger with a sigh.

Trying to put a positive spin on her situation she said, "Look at it this way, Cassie, with no need to work at the bakery, we'll have a lot more time to dedicate to tracking down Kevin's killer."

Chapter Seven

Lexy pulled up in front of McGreevy funeral home at 4:15 on the dot. Kevin's wake had started at 4:00 but the parking lot was already packed full. She maneuvered her VW bug into an end slot which seemed barely wide enough for the small car.

Rummaging in her glove compartment, she pulled out a lint roller. Gingerly stepping out of the car, she brushed white dog hairs from her black and gray pinstripe skirt, then tossed the roller back in through the open door before closing it. Smoothing her cream colored blouse, she surveyed herself in the window of her car. Satisfied with her appearance, she walked towards the gigantic glass and oak doors, her understated black Manolo Blahnik platform shoes making soft tapping sounds on the asphalt.

Two dark suited men opened the doors for her. Stepping inside, she was surrounded by the somber energy of the grieving. Hushed conversation, barely audible hymnal music and the faint scent of flowers filled the air of the tastefully decorated century old mansion.

Lexy followed the signs to a room on the left. The casket was just to the right of the door. She reluctantly glanced at it, her stomach lurching uncomfortably at seeing Kevin laying so still inside. Even though she had no love loss for him, she certainly didn't wish him dead. Seeing him laying in there made her heart clench. Her eyes pricked with unexpected tears. She had loved him once, no matter what he had done, he didn't deserve this

The sound of loud sobs to the left pulled her attention from the casket. She looked over, her eyes drawn to a gorgeous, and expensive, pair of red Stuart Weitzman shoes on the feet of an attractive bleached blonde who was crying uncontrollably into a tissue. *Who the heck is that?* Clearly she must have known Kevin well to be so upset, but Lexy had never seen her before.

"Lexy, thank you so much for coming." Jason appeared at her elbow. His eyes were red rimmed with big dark circles underneath.

"Oh, Jason... I'm so sorry." Lexy reached over to hug him. Jason grabbed on to her like a drowning man. He hugged her, a little tighter, and a little longer, than she felt comfortable with. Pungent pine scented aftershave filled her nostrils and when he finally released her she couldn't help but breathe a sigh of relief.

He pulled her over to the corner, away from the main crowd. He leaned in close, Lexy noticed the intent look in his eye. "Did Kevin try to contact you, maybe tell you something or give you something?" His voice was low, barely above a whisper.

Lexy was taken aback by his question, she felt her eyebrows knitting together in confusion. "No," she shook her head. "Why would he contact *me*? I haven't seen him since the breakup."

"Oh." Jason's face went blank. "He'd been acting a little funny lately - he mentioned you a couple of times..." He let his voice trail off.

"That's strange." Lexy's mind was racing. *Kevin had mentioned her?*

"Lexy, I'm sorry you got dragged into this mess with your cupcakes and all, I'm sure its just a coincidence."

"Yes, of course," Lexy said. "Thanks. I know the police will clear it up in no time. Have they told you anything?" Lexy felt like a jerk, pumping Jason for information at his brother's wake, but getting her bakery opened and clearing herself was her top priority.

"Nothing," he said, "what about you?"

Lexy shook her head.

"If you hear anything, will you let me know right away?"

"Of course." Lexy no sooner got the words out then a wail echoed through the room. Lexy figured it was the woman in the red shoes. Out of curiosity she asked Jason "Who is the woman over there in the red shoes?"

"Oh, that's my assistant, Sheila - her and Kevin were dating. She's pretty broke up about this since they had a bit of a falling out before Kevin...well...you know."

A falling out? Lexy thought back to some of the fallings out she had with Kevin. There were times she felt like she could have killed him. Of course, she never would have gone through with it, but maybe Sheila had a darker side.

An older man in an expensive suite came up to Jason interrupting Lexy from asking just how much of a falling out Kevin had had with the girl. Lexy recognized him as some important town official.

"Excuse me," Jason said to Lexy turning his full attention to the older man.

Lexy drifted off into the next room, her eyes scanning for familiar faces. A room with refreshments was setup off to the side, it was empty so Lexy wandered in - as much to get away from the crowd as to sample some of the food.

The table had an array of delicious looking cookies, from a bakery - not hers though she noted grimly. She picked a small almond frosted cookie. Taking a dainty bite she chewed it thoughtfully thinking back to what Jason had said about Kevin mentioning her. *Why would Kevin be talking about her?* Suddenly, she felt someone behind her.

She turned. The man was standing barely six inches from her face. His outfit looked to be about 15 years old - like it was the one "good" outfit he had which he wore to all such occasions. He smelled like booze, his chin dotted with day old stubble. His dark, beady eyes drilled into hers. There was something vaguely familiar about him, but Lexy couldn't quite place it.

Lexy's breath caught in her throat, the dry cookie crumbs tearing a cough from her chest.

"You'd do best to leave things alone." His voice was soft and low. Lexy had to turn her car towards him to hear.

"Excuse me?" Lexy felt a surge of panic. *Who was this guy?*

"I know who you are. I was real close to Kevin. I know things. Just take my advice and mind your own business." He spoke quickly, in short sentences his eyes darting around the room.

Lexy felt her eyes grow wide. "You know why Kevin was murdered?"

She blurted it out without thinking. The man backed away from her in a hurry. Beating a hasty retreat out of the room, he threw one last warning over his shoulder, “Stay out of it, or you’ll be sorry.”

Lexy dropped her cookie on the table, starting after the man but he had disappeared. She scanned the adjoining room, standing on her tip toes to get a good view but she didn’t see him anywhere. Who she did see, though, was the last person she wanted to run into. Detective Jack Perillo.

***

Jack stood in the corner, watching the people at Kevin’s wake. He had given his condolences to the family but he always liked to hang around for a while to observe the behavior of the people attending. In his experience you could find out more by watching what people did rather than listening to what they said.

Sudden, sporadic movements in the adjoining room caught his attention. He felt his eyes narrow when he recognized who was making the commotion, it was Lexy Baker bouncing up and down on her toes, apparently looking for someone in the crowd. *What's she doing here?*

Jack caught Lexy's eye, giving a short wave. She didn't wave back. Instead, she turned away, skirting the edge of the crowd. She seemed to be making a bee-line for the back of the house.

From his vantage point, Jack saw Kevin's mother, Ellen, look at Lexy. He saw Elle's eyes growing big and round, her face turning an unhealthy shade of red. He watched her raise her arm, pointing at Lexy.

"What's *she* doing here?" Ellen's voice rang out through the entire funeral parlor. All conversation came to a halt. Heads swiveled towards the loud voice.

"She *killed* my Kevin!" The sentence ended in an anguished wail. Jack saw Ellen lunge toward Lexy who was standing frozen like a deer caught in the headlights.

Jack sprung into action, making his way over to the distraught woman in order to diffuse the situation. It was already turning into a free for all with two people holding Ellen back. Lexy stood against the wall looking as if she wished she could disappear into it. All eyes were on the two of them.

Jack took Ellen's arm. He addressed her in a soothing voice "Ellen, we don't know who the killer is. There's no evidence to say Lexy did it."

Ellen turned confused, angry eyes on him. "She was never any good for him. Always acting like she was better than him." Jack felt grateful she wasn't yelling anymore.

Jason appeared wrapping a soothing arm around his mother who dissolved into tears. Addressing the crowd, he said softly, "Mamma's under a lot of stress, she doesn't know what she is saying."

A sympathetic murmur ran through the crowd. Out of the corner of his eye, Jack saw Lexy start to back away. He released Ellen's arm, then took one long step towards Lexy. Grabbing her by the elbow, he propelled her towards the back door, her shorter legs moving at double speed to try to keep up with him.

***

“What are you doing here?” Jack demanded in a low voice.

“I wanted to give my condolences.” Jack could tell by her voice it wasn’t the only reason she was there. He felt his right eyebrow raise in question.

“Really - Jason and I have been friends for a long time and I knew Ellen pretty good.” Her look of innocence didn’t fool Jack but it did distract him. His thoughts turning to her pouty lips and wide eyes instead of on the investigation at hand.

“Yes, it seems she was a big fan of yours,” Jack said sarcastically.

“She never really did warm to me. I guess no one was good enough for her little boy.” Lexy’s soft, green eyes looked up into his causing Jacks heart to melt a little. “Thanks for sticking up for me in there.”

Jack nodded in response. He looked down at her, the detective in him wanted to ask more questions about why she was at the wake to find out if she knew something about the case. The man in him wanted an excuse to spend more time with her. He quickly came up with a way to satisfy them both.

"Have you eaten supper yet?"

Lexy looked at her watch. "I haven't eaten since breakfast... I guess I *am* kind of hungry."

"Great, lets go to my favorite place and grab a burger." Jack threw the invitation out casually as if it was no big deal wondering why, if it really *was* no big deal, did he feel so nervous.

He saw Lexy hesitate. He thought she might be about to say no, but after a second she smiled. "Sure, why not. Maybe you can tell me more about your progress on the case and let me know when I can finally get my business opened."

"Great, we can take my car and then I'll drop you back here after." He set off towards the corner of the parking lot and Lexy followed. Leading her over to the passenger side of his Ford SUV, he opened the door for her watching her climb in. He glanced appreciatively at her curvy calfs as she pulled them up into the cab, his glance lingering long enough to notice her stiletto heeled shoes. His provocative thoughts about her shapely calves were interrupted, his mind going back to the crime scene and the unmistakable heel prints left around Kevin's house.

Chapter Eight

Ten minutes later, they were seated in a cozy booth at the Burger Barn, a family restaurant located in an old renovated barn. Jack liked the quaint atmosphere. Antique signs and farm memorabilia decorated the barn board walls and the lighting was moderate - not too dim and not too bright. The seating was comfortable and the burgers were the best in town.

Jack glanced over at Lexy. Judging by the way she was shoveling her burger into her mouth, she either agreed they were delicious or she hadn't eaten in a very long time.

"Good burgers," he said, smiling at the gob of ketchup she had on the side of her mouth. "You have some ketchup here..." he pointed to the side of his mouth with his finger.

"Oh!" Lexy picked up a napkin and swiped at the side of her mouth. "Thanks." She mumbled around her mouthful of burger, her face taking on a sheepish grin.

"They are good," she agreed after finishing up her bite. She picked up a sweet potato fry and nibbled on the end. "So, *detective*, is there anything more you can tell me about the case?"

Jack looked over at her smiling at him from across the table. *Hey shouldn't I be asking the questions?*

"Well, I can't talk to much about the details but I do know they are sifting through the ingredients from your bakery now. You should be able to open soon." Jack's answer seemed mechanical - impersonal. He mentally kicked himself for not being more entertaining.

Jack prided himself on being a good conversationalist. He was usually able to charm any woman on a date. But this wasn't a date. *Did he want it to be?* No, he definitely didn't want it to be a date. He just wanted to find out what Lexy knew about Kevin's murder. He got the distinct impression she knew something he didn't.

Jack had to admit he felt a strong attraction to Lexy, but dating just wasn't in the cards for him. His work was his main focus and women just seemed to get in the way of that. His last girlfriend had dumped him because he spent too much time at work and not enough time with her and he just didn't need *that* to happen again with Lexy especially since her house was practically right in his back yard.

"What about a motive?" Lexy's question pulled Jack's attention back to the table.

"Motive? You sound like you've been brushing up on detective-speak." Jack said with a laugh.

"Well, the murderer must have had a *reason* to do what they did."

"Sure." He put on his most charming smile." Of course, you have the usual reasons - jealousy, anger, revenge."

"But this was premeditated, so it wasn't a ... what do they call it?" Lexy looked up and bit her lower lip searching for the term. Jack could almost see the lightbulb go off over her head as she remembered it. "Crime of passion!"

"Sure, so it wasn't a spur of the moment thing. It must have been something someone planned. Do you know anyone who would have a reason for wanting Kevin dead so much they would plan it?" Jack tried to slip the question in casually to catch her off guard, just in case she did have some idea who did it.

"No, do you?" She smiled at him sweetly. Jack could have sworn she was batting her eyelashes. *Was she flirting with him?* Jack was surprised to discover he didn't mind if she was.

Jack decided to throw Lexy a little bone in the hopes she might reciprocate. "We haven't come up with much, but we do know Kevin may have been involved in some sort of blackmail scheme."

"Blackmail?" Lexy looked perplexed. "Who in the world would he be blackmailing?"

"If we knew *that*," Jack said, "then we'd already have our killer."

Lexy looked deep in thought, after a few seconds she said, "A strange man threatened me at the wake today."

Jack leaned forward, listening intently. This could be the clue he was looking for. "What did he say?"

"He warned me not to mess around looking for Kevin's killer. He said if I did I'd be sorry." Jack could see Lexy give a little shiver as she said the last words.

"What did he look like? Did you get his name? How did he know Kevin?" Jack slipped into detective mode, rattling off the questions in quick order.

"He looked disheveled. He wore rumpled clothes and he hadn't shaved in days. Medium height, dark hair with a tinge of gray. He seemed nervous. Honestly, it all happened so fast I didn't find out anything about him except he said he knew Kevin well."

"Oh." Jack was a little disappointed with the lack of information, but interested at least someone out there had answers, now it was up to Jack to try to find him.

Jack looked over at Lexy, his face becoming serious. "Lexy, you'd be smart to heed that guys warning. Messing around in this case could be very dangerous. I hope you're not taking things into your own hands?"

"Oh, no... I wouldn't know the first thing about looking for a murderer." Lexy said.

Jack felt his eyes narrow, she sounded a little too sincere, he thought. He didn't think she was lying to him...not exactly...but he did get the distinct impression Lexy Baker was crossing her fingers behind her back when she implied she wouldn't be meddling in the investigation.

***

They rode back to the funeral parlor in comfortable silence. Lexy was surprised, and a bit dismayed, to discover she had enjoyed Jack's company.

She'd even liked flirting with him, although she told herself it was to try to get information. It had paid off too because now, at least, the blackmail angle gave her something to go on. She felt a little bad about not telling Jack that Kevin had been asking about her but she figured it might not be smart to tell him things which could cast suspicion on *her*.

Jack parked near her car, then jumped out to open the door for her. They walked over to her car slowly, enjoying the warm summer evening, the sound of peepers chirping filled the honeysuckle scented air.

Lexy unlocked her car turning to face Jack "Thanks for supper. I can't believe I've never been there before - the food is wonderful!"

"You're welcome," Jack said, then reached into his pocket producing the key to her bakery. "Here's your key. I'm sorry about having to keep your bakery closed."

Lexy reached out to retrieve the key and her fingers brushed his as she took it, causing a tingle of excitement.

Lexy looked up at him, her stomach flip flopped at the way he was looking at her with his gorgeous golden brown eyes. *Was he going to kiss her?*

Jack leaned in towards her. She felt her breath catch in her throat. His lips met hers. Soft. Casual.

Lexy snaked an arm around his neck, pressing her body closer, wanting more. She felt his strong arms around her waist, pulling her in tighter. His lips pressing harder. His tongue probing.

The shrill ring of Jacks cell phone broke the spell. He pulled away, wrenching the phone from is pocket.

"Hello," he barked the greeting into the phone. "Yes. Where. Darling, I'll be there."

He turned to Lexy. "I'm sorry, I have to go out on a call. I'll call you later." The last sentence was more a question than a statement.

Lexy, managed a nod, still too breathless from the kiss to speak. She watched him get in his car and speed off.

Lexy stood in the parking lot for a moment, her lips still burning from his kiss. *What the heck had she been thinking?*

Even though she couldn't deny the warm, tingly glow she felt when she was near him, kissing the handsome detective could add a bunch of complications to her life which she just didn't need now - and who had he called *darling* on the phone?

Her eyelid started to twitch nervously. The last thing Lexy needed was to get involved with a guy who had a girlfriend. Better to keep her hormones in check and stay away from Detective Jack Perillo.

She hopped in her car. Being in an empty funeral parlor parking lot at night creeped her out. She couldn't help but think of the man she had talked to at the wake. She wasn't sure what he had meant or if his words were a warning intended to keep her safe or a threat intended to scare her off.

Chapter Nine

Lexy slipped into her chair delicately balancing a chocolate croissant in one hand and a caramel latte in the other. She glanced around the room in the contemporary style cafe noting the modern purple and green colors, comfortable booth seating and scrolly architecture design. *Maybe she should get more comfortable chairs for the Cup and Cake?*

A heavy sigh escaped her lips at the thought of her bakery, wondering how long it would be until she could open it again and if being closed would hurt business. Having to buy all new ingredients wasn't helping her bank account any. She felt a rush of anger at the police department.

"Why so glum?" Cassie slid into the other side of the booth.

"Oh, I was just thinking about the bakery and wondering when we can open again." Lexy said, her heart feeling a slight squeeze at her predicament.

Cassie nodded in sympathy, dipping her tea bag into a steaming cup of water. “Maybe what I found out from Tom McGraw will cheer you up, then.”

Lexy raised her eyebrows. “You talked to him? What did he say?”

“He said Kevin had been acting a little cagey lately - withdrawn. He also said it looked like Kevin had come into some money but he was keeping pretty quiet about it.”

“Really? That’s interesting because last night Jack said they thought Kevin might have been involved in some sort of blackmail scheme.” Lexy thought back to the previous night feeling her cheeks grow hot at the memory of Jack’s kiss.

“Jack?” Cassie raised a pierced eyebrow.

“Detective Perillo. I saw him at the wake and then talked to him...after.”

“Oh, that hunky detective who came to the bakery?” Cassie’s eyes narrowed. “Wait a minute, you’re being kind of cagey yourself - what’s going on?”

Lexy rolled her eyes. Her old friend could always tell when she was trying to hide something from her. “There’s nothing *going on.* I saw him at the wake and we grabbed a burger. Did I mention he is also my neighbor?”

“He is? You forgot to mention that. So have you known him long? You never said anything about him before.” Lexy saw Cassie’s mouth form a smirk, she knew her friend was picturing a romance between Lexy and Jack.

“No, actually I met him the night before he came to the bakery. I saw him at the wake and took my opportunity to get information from him.” Lexy said nonchalantly, purposely leaving out the part about the kiss. “Anyway, I think he has a girlfriend.”

“Oh, too bad. All the good ones seem to be taken.” Cassie said with a sigh. “So, anyway, did you find out anything at the wake?”

Lexy told Cassie about what she had learned. How Jason said Kevin had mentioned her. How the woman with the expensive red shoes had been balling her eyes out. And the warning from the disheveled man. When she got to the last part, she saw Cassie's eyes widen and heard her take a sharp breath.

"Oh Lexy, you better be careful! Maybe looking into this stuff isn't such a good idea." Cassie said, concern softening her jet black eyes.

"Oh, I'll be careful." Lexy's heart warmed at her friends care, she didn't want her to worry. Even though Cassie looked tough on the outside, she was a marshmallow on the inside. "Besides, once the bakery is opened I can just drop the whole thing. That's all I really care about."

"Speaking of which," Lexy added. "Can you remember who might have bought cupcakes tops the day Kevin died? The murderer must have come in to the shop to buy the cupcake tops - or sent someone in to get them."

Both girls were silent for a few minutes trying to remember.

"It's so hard to remember," Cassie said. "Every day seems to just blend into each other. I know we have the regulars, but I don't remember anyone who would stand out.... Wait! I do remember someone who seemed a little off...he smelled like booze and looked a little grungy. I remember wondering why someone like that would want cupcakes."

Lexy thought back to the man at the wake - he had smelled like booze. "The man who threatened me at the wake smelled like booze.... I also remember seeing someone with expensive shoes come in, but I can't remember what day. I didn't get a good look at her though - I was too busy admiring the shoes."

"I guess thats not much to go on either way." Lexy said, feeling disappointment settle in her stomach like a heavy brick.

She shoved the last piece of croissant in her mouth. "I guess we should get going. I need to get to the bakery and accept the deliveries so we can restock the pantry. Nans called - she wants me to come over later to update the ladies on our progress," she said with a wry smile.

Lexy felt like they hadn't made much progress at all. Sure, they had a few clues but Lexy didn't feel like they were any closer to finding the killer or getting her bakery open. She felt anxious and scared, she looked forward to meeting with Nans later that day. Maybe the Ladies Detective Club would have made better progress then her and Cassie.

Chapter Ten

Lexy got out of her car in the parking lot of the Brook Ridge Retirement community center in a cloud of flour dust. She'd spent the afternoon at the bakery waiting for delivery men and logging and stocking ingredients. Somehow she'd gotten flour all over her black tee-shirt and jeans. She batted at her clothing to try to brush it all off.

Lexy opened the door to the community area. Nans came rushing over to greet her.

"Lexy - we've get something very interesting to talk to you about!" Nans grabbed Lexy's hand, pulling her over to the round table where the women from the Ladies Detective Club were waiting.

"Good to see you too, Nans." Lexy's sarcastic smile made Nans laugh.

"Sorry dear." Nans gave Lexy a hug. "Of course, its always wonderful to see you. Now sit." She pointed towards an empty chair.

Nans, whipped out her iPad. Placing it on the table, she turned it so Lexy could see the screen. The women leaned in towards the center of the table excitedly.

"We found something that might be a clue." Nans said in a hushed whisper, her eyes dramatically darting from side to side, her fingers deftly clicked the icons on the tablet.

Lexy looked down at the image of a newspaper page, the headline read *Bridge Repair Fund Missing Money*. "A news story?" She looked up at Nans.

Nans nodded. "The story says a government project to repair bridges has been found to have funds missing. The project is one of Jason's pet projects. Read it and you'll see for yourself."

Lexy picked up the iPad to read the story while the ladies watched her in anticipatory silence.

Putting the iPad down, Lexy bit her bottom lip. "This *is* interesting, but it says they don't know where the moncy went. I mean it could just be lost in the system."

"Or someone could have embezzled it. Maybe somehow Kevin was involved - being Jason's brother he might have had an in - and *that's* what got him killed." Ida interjected from the other side of the table. The other women nodded in agreement.

"But why use my cupcakes to do it?"

"Probably just a coincidence. Poison is a non violent way to kill someone and you are the only bakery in town..." Nans let the sentence trail off.

"Now, tell us what *you* found out at the wake." Nans leaned closer, her eyes as big as saucers.

Amidst a chorus of gasps and oh's, Lexy told them how Jason had told her Kevin had been asking about her. She told them about the woman with the expensive shoes who was Jason's assistant and also dating Kevin. She purposely omitted the part about the man warning her off because she didn't want Nans to worry. Finally she told them how Jack had mentioned something about blackmail.

"Aha! That's it," Nans put her fist in the air. "Kevin was blackmailing whoever took the money from the fund!"

"...or Kevin took the money and someone was blackmailing him..." Ida said.

"The crying woman is interesting. You said she's Jason's assistant? I wonder how she can afford those shoes." Ruth said matter of factly.

"You know," Helen said, "I remember seeing an episode of *Murder She Wrote*, or maybe it was *Columbo*, where the murderer was the secretary who had been embezzling money and had to kill the sister who found out about it, maybe it was the assistant. That would explain how she could buy expensive shoes."

"Now don't forget she was Kevin's girlfriend too." Nans said.

Lexy's head was spinning with all the possibilities. She felt her heart sinking. *Now there were too many suspects!*

"It seems like there are a few possibilities to explore now." Lexy felt a little overwhelmed. *How would she narrow it down to the killer?* "But we are making a big assumption the missing funds have something to do with the murder. It could be something else entirely."

Nans gave her a knowing look. "Dear, trust me, we've been doing this for a while now - we know when something *feels* right. And this feels right. Doesn't it, girls?"

Lexy looked around the table. The women nodded their agreement with all the confidence of seasoned detectives.

Lexy stood, a heavy sigh escaping her lips. "Thanks for the information, ladies. I guess I have a lot to think about now."

"It's all in a days work!" Nans said, then added, "We're happy to help. But do be careful, dear. Don't do any detective work on your own - if you need to do something dangerous, call Jack Perillo first."

The mischievous glint in Nans' eye was not lost on Lexy. She chose to ignore it. Bidding the women good evening, she turned towards the door hoping for a non-eventful ride home where she could spend a relaxing evening with a good glass of wine and Sprinkles at her side.

***

Lexy pulled into her driveway. She felt exhausted, everything that had happened the past few days was starting to take it's toll. A glance at her overflowing mailbox reminded her she had forgotten all about taking the mail in.

She grabbed the pile of mail, clutching it to her chest. Wrestling with the keys, she managed to get the door open without dropping the mail. As usual, Sprinkles was there to greet her. Lexy bent down to pet the dog, then crossed the living room to the kitchen, tossing the pile of mail on the table.

A strange looking manilla envelope slid out to the side. Lexy picked it up, perplexed as to what it could be - she didn't remember ordering anything.

She recognized the handwriting on the front and her heart froze. It was Kevin's writing.

Lexy threw the envelope down, backing away, She felt fear zinging through her body like an electric current. *Why would Kevin send her a package*?

Lexy was torn - curious to see what was inside, but afraid at the same time. Tentatively she reached out for the envelope, touching it gingerly as if it might bite her.

She sat down, perched on the edge of her chair, the envelope in her hands. Slowly she slid a perfectly manicured nail under the flap, tearing it open. She tipped it upside down. A small, blue notebook slid out onto the table.

Lexy took a deep breath. Picking up the notebook, she opened it to the first page. She felt her brow furrow when she saw what it was - just a jumble of numbers with what looked like dates and words that looked like they were in code. *What the heck is this?*

Lexy peered back inside the envelope. It was empty, no note or other communication to tell her what the notebook was about. She leafed through the book, but there was nothing in there to tell her what it was just page after page of numbers and garbled words.

She sat back blowing out a rush of air through pursed lips. *Now what?* Clearly, the book had something to do with Kevin's murder. If only she could figure out what all the numbers and words meant.

With a start Lexy realized having the book could be dangerous. What if the killer knew Kevin had this book and figured out he had mailed it to her? Lexy felt anxiety gnaw at her stomach, she had to get rid of it.

She knew the book should be in the hands of the police. Sneaking a peek out her kitchen window, she could see lights on at Jack's house. Much as she wanted to avoid him, she knew she should give him the book right away.

She jumped up from her chair, her mind made up. She went out the back door shooing Sprinkles inside when she tried to follow. Crossing her yard, she wriggled through the gap in the fence popping out the other side in Jack's yard.

Lexy felt butterflies start swarming in her stomach and it wasn't because she was nervous about the book. She couldn't deny she felt excited about seeing Jack again. Try as she might, she couldn't get last nights kiss out of her mind. She felt a warm glow below her stomach. *Cripes! Stop acting like a hormone rattled teenager and just give him the damn book!*

She started up the slope to Jacks house but what she saw in his living room window made her stop short. Silhouetted in the window were two figures talking and laughing. One was Jack. The other one had long curly hair. *His girlfriend?*

Lexy felt a ball of anger in the pit of her stomach. He had kissed her just last night. Tonight, he has another woman at his house. She knew she didn't have any claim on Jack, after all it was just a kiss not a commitment, but she felt cheated just the same.

Maybe it was because of the hurt she had felt when Kevin had cheated on her, maybe she was overly sensitive, but whatever the reason, she was too mad to go to Jacks house now. She turned abruptly. Scurrying back through the fence, she crossed the yard to her kitchen, slamming the door shut behind her.

Chapter Eleven

Lexy woke up at the crack of dawn in a tangle of sheets. She had barely slept all night. Her head felt like someone was trying to jackhammer cement inside it.

After her excursion in the backyard, she had called Cassie looking for advice on what to do with the notebook, but Cassie didn't answer. Lexy had ended up hiding it in the best hiding spot she could think of - Sprinkles dog bed.

Sprinkles didn't seem to mind at all. She was leaping around with her usual morning energy Wagging her tail, she stared adoringly at Lexy. Lexy couldn't help but smile at the little dog.

"You don't have any other girlfriends *and* love me no matter what, huh, girl?" She stroked the dog's fur, then swinging her legs over the bed, got up to face the day.

Lexy caught her reflection in the mirror, a groan escaping her lips when she saw the dark circles under her eyes. It was going to take some strong coffee and a long, hot shower to get her ready to face the day.

She padded downstairs in her bare feet. Lifting the cushion off Sprinkles dog bed, she ran her finger along the edge of the seam, feeling for the gap in the stitches. She poked her finger inside, feeling the hard edge of the notebook. Satisfied it was still there, she pushed the sides back together and replaced the cushion.

She was about halfway into her coffee starting to feel alive again when her cell phone sounded.

"Hello?"

"Hi, I saw you called last night." Lexy recognized Cassie's voice.

"You won't believe this. Remember how Jason asked if Kevin had contacted me?"

"Yes..."

"Well, I got a package in the mail from Kevin yesterday." Talking about it made Lexy realize the implications of having the notebook. She felt a heavy cloud of foreboding settle in her stomach.

"A package?"

"It was a notebook, with cryptic writing in it ... I have no idea what it means. Want to come over and take a look?"

"Ughh, I can't" Cassie's disappointed voice rang through the phone. "Can you send me some pictures of the pages? Maybe I can figure something out."

"Sure, I can. I'll hang up and send them right away."

"OK, I'll call you later then."

Lexy went over to the dog bed, taking a quick peek out the windows to make sure no one would interrupt her. She slipped the book out of it's hiding place. Snapping off a few photos with her smartphone, she sent them to Cassie, then put the book back.

The cell phone went off in her hands. It was Nans.

"Hi Nans. I have some breaking news. Something big."

"Oh really, what?"

"I got a package in the mail yesterday ... it was from Kevin." Lexy could hear a sharp intake of breath from the other end of the phone.

"What was it?"

"It was a notebook, but I can't make out what it says. It seems to be in code or something. I have some pictures of the pages - I can bring them over if you want."

"That would be great! Ida is somewhat of a cryptographer, maybe she can figure out what it all means."

"OK, great. I'll be over in a bit." Lexy closed the phone. Fumbling to put it in her purse, she knocked it over. The contents spilled out on the floor.

Sprinkles jumped on Lexy's shiny key ring, batting it around until it disappeared under the radiator.

"Oh, Sprinkles! Sheesh." Lexy took a deep breath, then let it out in a loud sigh. She got down on her hands and knees to reach under the radiator - she felt the cold metal of the keys with her fingertips and pulled. They didn't budge - they were stuck!

Laying flat on the hard, linoleum floor, she reached her arm even further in to grab a better hold. She wrestled with the keys, pulling this way and tugging that way. Finally, her efforts were rewarded and the keys came loose. Lexy held them up in front of her face - she had a large amount of keys but they appeared to be all accounted for. She dropped them in her purse, then hurried upstairs to shower and get ready to go to Nans.

***

Lexy sat at the table in the Brook Ridge Retirement community center, the Ladies Detective Club clustered around her. She brought up the pictures on her smart phone passing it around so everyone could get a look. The actual book was still hidden in Sprinkles bed - Lexy didn't feel comfortable carrying it around with her.

Ruth and Helen quickly flipped through the pictures, Ida spent a longer time looking at them.

“It looks like a substitution cypher,” Ida squinted at the small pictures, scribbling something down on a notepad. “But it could take a long time to figure out the code without the key. Did you get anything else with the notebook?”

“No, there was nothing else in the envelope.”

“Well, this proves one thing,” Nans said. “Kevin must have been blackmailing someone.”

“Yeah, but who ... and what about.”

“The answer to that,” Ida said, tapping the smart phone with the tip of her pencil. “Is right here in the book. We just need to figure it out.”

“Lexy, you need to get this book to the police right away.” Nans mouth was set in a grim line, her eyes deadly serious. “It looks like Kevin got killed for this information - for what he knows. And now you know it too. You could be in grave danger.”

***

Lexy was jittery. She didn't want to go home, so she opted for a trip to the mall. Shoe shopping always made her feel better, plus she could use the distraction to clear her head and help her think better.

She knew Nans was right about the book. Paging through the caller list on her phone she found Jacks number. She clicked on it, listening to the hollow ring on the other end, her stomach a jangle of nerves. He didn't answer. *Now what?* She left a short message asking him to call her.

Zipping into a parking spot at the front of the mall, she hopped out of her car, making a beeline for her favorite shoe store. Staring at the racks of designer shoes soothed Lexy's mind. She picked out a purple suede platform pair, a black and rhinestones dressy stiletto pair, and a couple of lower heeled sandals to try on.

Sexy red shoes caught her eye. She thought back to the woman at the wake - Kevin's girlfriend. *Did she have something to do with it?*

Ruth was right, those shoes sold for $500 - $1000 and an assistants salary didn't allow for such luxuries.

Of course, Kevin could have bought them for her with his blackmail money.

Or she could be the embezzler...or the blackmailer.

For all she knew, Kevin was the embezzler and someone was blackmailing *him*.

And why did Jason ask if Kevin had contacted her? Was he involved too, did he know Kevin was going to send the book?

Who was the grungy man that had warned her off? Maybe he was in on it with the embezzler and didn't want her to find out the truth.

How would she ever figure out who the real killer was? Lexy sat down hard on the bench to try on her shoes. She needed a good solid lead pointing to one of the suspects. That, and a nice new pair of shoes would make everything all better.

***

After trying on what seemed like a hundred pairs, Lexy was exhausted. A glance at her watch told her it was nearing suppertime. Jack still hadn't returned her call.

Dragging several packages along with her, she navigated the nearly full parking lot to her car. The hell with Detective Jack Perillo, if he didn't think her phone call was important, then he could wait to find out she had the notebook. Sprinkles needed to be fed and let out so she headed home, danger or no danger.

At her front door, Lexy balanced her packages while she searched the key ring for her key. *Damn! It wasn't there!* She remembered how the ring had gotten stuck under the radiator earlier that morning. The front door key must have fallen off in the struggle.

Remembering there was a spare key for the kitchen door under the planter in the back, Lexy set off around the side of the house. She could hear Sprinkles barking inside. The poor dog wasn't used to Lexy walking around to the back. Sprinkles probably thought she was an intruder. Lexy felt herself smile with pride that her little watchdog was trying to protect the house.

In the back, Lexy put down her packages. Bending down she lifted the planter with both hands. It was almost dark, but the key glinted in the fading sunlight. She balanced the planter against her hip, grabbed the key with one had, then replaced the planter gently.

Turning to the door, she put the key in the lock, twisted the knob and pushed the door open. A sudden rustle of movement to her right caught her attention. She turned to see what it was. A sharp, hard pain exploded in the back of her head. For a split second, she felt the sensation of falling...and then there was nothing but darkness.

Chapter Twelve

Lexy dug her toes in the sand. She was laying on the beach, the warm water lapping at her cheek. Jack was next to her holding her hand. She had the feeling he was about to ask a very important question.

"Lexy..."

"Umm hmmm..." She mumbled, not wanting to disturb her perfectly positioned, bikini clad body. She turned her head to face Jack. He looked good with no shirt on. *Very* good.

She felt a light slap on her cheek, the sand feeling unusually hard under her, the smell of pine permeating her nostrils. *Pine? Wait a minute, shouldn't she be smelling the salty sea air?*

"Lexy!"

She opened her eyes, but instead of seeing a beautiful tropical beach, she saw her kitchen from an odd angle. Sprinkles face hovered over hers, her little tongue enthusiastically lapping at her cheek.

"Wha...?"

"Lexy, are you OK?" Jack's voice broke through her confusion. She turned to face him, her head pounding, her beach dream evaporating into reality.

"Yes. I think so. What happened? Why am I on the floor?"

"I don't know, I happened to notice you laying here like this from my window." Jack pointed over to his house where his living room window had a clear view to Lexy's back door.

Lexy started to sit up, but it felt like she was glued to the floor. Jack slipped an arm around her to help her. She leaned against him. It felt nice to have someone to take care of her. For a split second she felt content ... until she looked around her kitchen. It was ransacked!

"Oh my God! What happened?" She felt her eyes narrow as she looked around the room, then at Jack.

"That's what I was going to ask you," he said, "it looks like someone was looking for something."

Lexy looked around, her heart dropping in her chest at what she saw. Drawers were pulled out, cabinets opened, stuff thrown on the floor. She must have been out like a light not to have heard the commotion.

"Do you know what they might have been looking for?" Jack persisted.

The notebook!

Lexy pushed herself away from Jack. She jumped up. Fighting off a wave of nausea and dizziness, she ran to the dog bed. Throwing the cushion on the floor, she jammed her hand inside the hole in the lining. *It was still there!*

She pulled her hand out clutching the book.

"I assume it was this." She thrust the book at Jack who had stood and taken a few steps towards her. Reaching out, he took the book from her.

Jack leafed through the book, his eyes growing wider at each page. "Where did you get this?"

"It came in the mail ... from Kevin."

"How long have you had this? Why didn't you tell me about it?" Jack stared down at her, his eyes dark with anger.

Lexy felt her cheeks grow warm, she looked away. Her surge of embarrassment at keeping the book was short lived when she remembered she had *tried* to tell Jack about it, but he never answered her call.

"I called you about this earlier today. I got it last night, but it might have been in the mailbox a day or two. You never returned my call." She stared him down, her annoyance hanging in the air between them.

"This is important evidence in the case." Jack held the book up.

Duh. Lexy stared at him. *Did he think she was stupid?*

"This book could hold the key to who the killer is." Jack stated the obvious. "And you could be in a lot of danger if the killer knows you have it. Clearly he or she already suspects you might. They've gone to a lot of trouble here to try to find it." He spread his arms indicating the mess in her kitchen, his anger turning to concern.

His concern diffused her annoyance and Lexy felt a sigh escape her lips. “I know.” She felt her heart beat a little faster. This *was* serious business, after all someone had knocked her out!

“Did you get a look at who hit you?”

“No.” Lexy’s hand went up to the back of her head. She felt a big lump starting to from. “They hit me from behind.”

Jack stepped closer. Moving behind her, he gently touched her hair, feeling the back of her head. Moving her hair aside he inspected the wounded area. “That’s a nasty lump, you should have it looked at. You might have a concussion. Do you want me to call an ambulance?”

Lexy shook her head. She knew that even if she did have a concussion, there was little they could do about it. An ambulance would just be a waste of time and money.

She saw Jacks eyes soften. He reached for her, tentatively pulling her in for a hug. For a split second, she let herself relax, letting out a soft sigh.

Then, remembering the curly haired woman in his window, she felt her body stiffen.

Jack broke the embrace. Clearing his throat he said, "I better get this book to the station so we can decipher it." He held the book up.

"Right." Lexy nodded. She felt a whirlwind of emotions. Part of her wanted to rush into Jacks arms and beg him to protect her, but the other part was sending up warning signals about his girlfriend. She straightened her spine, willing herself to be strong and independent. She tried to keep a cool, nonchalant look on her face, even though she was a little spooked that someone had knocked her out and tossed her house.

Jack walked to the edge of the kitchen, peeking into the other rooms. "It looks like they've been through your house pretty good. I'm going to station a car outside overnight, just in case they come back. I don't think they will, but you might want to go somewhere else tonight."

Lexy looked around. The house was a mess. She had a lot of work to do. She scooped Sprinkles up in her arms. "Thanks, but I think I'll stay here - I have

Sprinkles to protect me." She buried her face in the little dogs fur. Sprinkles wagged her tail, turning her head to lick Lexy's face.

"*Promise* me you'll take it easy - and call me if anything else happens!" Jack gave her a tender, concerned look that made Lexy's heart do flip flops.

"I promise." She held up her hand, the first two fingers up in the air, the rest folded. "Scouts honor."

Jack gave her one final glance, than disappeared out the back door.

Lexy collapsed into the closest kitchen chair with a sigh. Sprinkles pawed at her legs, blissfully unaware of the goings on.

"You're probably hungry, huh?"

Picking up the dog bowl, she crossed to the counter and pulled out Sprinkles canister of food. She filled the bowl, then put it on the floor. She expected Sprinkles to dig in as soon as she saw it, but something else had attracted the dog's attention.

Lexy watched Sprinkles push a shiny metal object across the floor, batting it from one side to the other.

"What's that, girl?" With the mess the house was in, it could be anything.

Lexy bent down, intercepting the item. She stood up, holding it in front of her face. It was a button. A rather distinctive button, gold in color with a black stone in the middle and Greek key scrolling on the outer edge.

Lexy felt her forehead wrinkle as she tried to remember whether she had an outfit with that style button. She didn't.

She felt her stomach drop, a chill ran up her spine when she realized it could mean only one thing - the button belonged to whoever had knocked her out and ransacked her house.

Chapter Thirteen

Lexy was up at the crack of dawn after another sleepless night. The presence of the police car outside her house gave her some peace of mind, but the real reason for her insomnia was the button.

Finally, she had the clue she had been looking for - the one that would lead her to Kevin's killer. Now all she had to do was figure out whose it was.

She fed Sprinkles, giving her an extra treat for finding the button, then jumped in the shower. She had a full day ahead of her and couldn't waste any time. Her first stop would be Nans so she could show the button to the Ladies Detective Club.

Forty-five minutes later she found herself seated at the usual round table in the retirement center telling the women about the previous nights events. The button sat in the center of the table, four blueish grey heads bent forward to inspect it.

"It's a lovely button," Ruth said.

"I can't say if it's a man's or a woman's," Ida added.

"It looks like it would come from an expensive blazer or dress," Helen said.

"Lexy," said Nans, "close your eyes and think back to the wake. Do you remember seeing anyone with a jacket that had these buttons?"

Lexy closed her eyes trying to picture Kevin's wake in her minds eye. Images of people floated through her mind, but she didn't see the button on any clothing. She probably wouldn't have noticed something like that anyway.

"Oh, look." Nans pointed at the big screen television on the other side of the room. "Isn't that Kevin's brother, Jason on TV?"

Lexy turned to look. It was Jason, standing at a podium giving some sort of speech. That wasn't anything out of the ordinary. He *was* the deputy mayor so he was often seen on TV. Lexy was about to turn away, then something on the TV caught her eye.

She stood, running over to the giant television, her eyes grew wide. She turned to the women at the table, feeling her cheeks flush with excitement.

"I think I know who the killer is!" She grabbed her purse, gave Nans a quick hug and rushed towards the door.

As she hit the door at full speed, she heard Nans panicked voice calling after her "Lexy, wait ... don't do anything dangerous on your own!"

***

"Kevin sent me something in the mail...it's a notebook." Lexy whispered into her cell phone.

"Do you have it? What does it say?" The familiar voice on the other end asked.

"It's in code so I don't know what it means, looks like some dates and garbled words."

She heard an audible sigh through the phone. "Can you bring it to me? I'd like to take a look at it." Lexy heard an edge of anxiety creep into the voice.

"Sure." She crossed her fingers behind her back. She didn't actually have the book anymore, but she had a plan to get a confession from the killer and the plan would only work if they met in person.

"OK, meet me at my house in 20 minutes," the voice on the other end said breathlessly into the phone.

Lexy snapped the phone shut. She rummaged in her glove compartment, pulling out a small tape recorder she kept to record any recipe ideas she might have and she slid it into her purse. A taped confession always worked on TV so she couldn't see why it wouldn't work for her. She found a little notebook in the back of her car that would work as a decoy. Finally, she pulled a can of pepper spray from under her seat just in case things got ugly.

Nans warning rang in her head. She *should* call Jack, but she knew he wouldn't approve of her plan and she couldn't wait any longer for the case to be solved so that her bakery could be open again. She was almost out of savings and needed to be earning money in order to pay her bills. Calling Jack would only slow things down.

Her decision made, she turned her cell phone off, then double checked her purse for the tape recorder, notebook and pepper spray. Satisfied everything was in order, she put her car in gear and drove off towards her destination.

Chapter Fourteen

Jack looked at his cell phone wondering if he should call Lexy to check on her. *No, better to wait a bit.*

He thought about the notebook she had given him last night. He had taken it to the station right away. His people were busy working on deciphering it. It should hold the clues which would point to whoever killed Kevin.

Which made him wonder what role Lexy had played, if any, in the whole thing. At first she was high up on their suspect list. But as the case unraveled, Jack was relieved to see it looked less and less like she had been involved.

Still, there were several things that pointed to her - the poison cupcake tops, her relationship with the deceased, and those stiletto heel marks weren't in her favor. But an intense investigation and surveillance hadn't turned anything else up. And, of course, last nights events pretty much cleared her...unless she had very cleverly staged it. But why would she give Jack the book? She *had* to be innocent, Jack thought, hoping his confidence in her innocence was because of the clues and evidence and not because of his feelings towards her.

Jack felt a sinking feeling in his stomach, if she was innocent, then her life could be in serious danger.

Jack's cell phone rang in his hand, startling him. He whipped it open, hoping it was Lexy.

"Jack! I hope you can help me... I'm worried about Lexy!"

"Mona?" Jack recognized Nans's voice.

"Yes, it's me. I think she may have gone off and done something stupid." Jack could hear the worry in Mona's voice.

"Take a deep breath and tell me what happened." Jack felt his heart clench.

"She was over here this morning. She found a button on her floor last night and assumed it was from whoever knocked her out so she came over to show it to us." Mona paused taking a deep, shaky breath.

"Go on." Jack knew there must be more to the story to get Mona so upset.

"Then, we were watching the TV when she suddenly announced she knew who the killer was and ran out!"

"Did she say where she was going? Or who she thought the killer was?"

"No, I tried to stop her but she was determined. I'm worried, I think she may be going to confront the killer herself!" Jack heard Mona's voice rise in panic.

"Don't worry, I'll find her." Jack said, struggling to keep his voice calm to stop the older woman from worrying. "I'll call you back as soon as I have her safe...you just sit tight, OK?"

"OK, thank you, Jack."

Jack snapped the phone shut. *Where could she have gone?*

He remembered the police car he had assigned to her. Were they still following her? He opened his phone punching the speed dial for the station with shaky fingers.

"Hi, this is Jack. Is that car still assigned to Lexy Baker?"

"No, we only had it booked for overnight." Jack felt his heart plummet. "But we do have some news on the notebook you brought in."

"Spill it."

"Moe's been able to decipher a little of it and all things point to our number one suspect."

"So, you think our theory was correct. Kevin caught him embezzling then started blackmailing him and was killed because of it?"

"Looks that way. But we still need something more concrete to arrest him."

Jack's mind flashed on what Mona had said about Lexy finding a button. "Let me call you back in a minute. I think I might have just what we need."

Jack looked through his recent calls, finding the one from Mona, he punched the button to call her back.

“Hi Mona, it’s Jack ... you said you were watching something on TV when Lexy announced she knew who the killer was, right?”

“Yes, that’s right.”

“Do you remember what you were watching?”

“Of course, it was Kevin’s brother Jason - you know he’s the deputy mayor, right? Well, anyway, he was on TV announcing something.”

Bingo!

“OK, thanks. I’ll call you soon.” Jack assured Mona, then disconnected the call and pressed the button to dial the station again.

“I have the hard evidence - a button from the killers jacket. Can we get a car out there right away?” Jack felt his heart beating faster. Lexy could be confronting the killer right now. Either way he was going there, but he’d feel a lot more confident if he had the whole police department behind him.

“Yep, I’ll put out the call right away. We’ll be ready to roll in about 10 minutes.” Jack felt a sigh of relief escape his lips. He snapped the phone shut and ran for his car.

Chapter Fifteen

Jason ushered Lexy hurriedly into the house, casting a glance outside before shutting the door.

"I knew you would come to me ... you didn't tell anyone else did you?"

"No, of course not." Lexy mentally crossed her fingers. She wanted Jason to feel like she was "on his side" so he'd be more apt to talk.

"Do you have the notebook?" Jason's stared at Lexy - she noticed his eyes were rimmed in red, his face wore a stubble of beard which was uncustomary for the clean cut politician.

Lexy took a few steps back. She reached into her purse, pulling out the book. She could feel her heart pounding with fear that Jason would know it wasn't the real one. Her eye started to twitch and she hoped the nervous reaction didn't give her away.

Jason ran his hands through his already unkempt hair, messing it up even more. "I can't believe Kevin did this to me. You understand why I had to do it, right? I did it for us."

Us? He must be delusional, Lexy thought. She gave what she hoped looked like an understanding nod of her head.

"I guess we have a lot in common, first Kevin betrays you and then me. But now we can be together, we can go anywhere we want with the money. I know you want to be together as badly as I do."

Go anywhere together? Lexy felt adrenalin cursing through her veins. Her flight reflexes ready to kick into gear. She knew Jason had wanted to be more than friends but she'd never given him any indication she wanted that too.

"The money? You mean from the bridge project?" She probed, trying to get him to come out and say it so she could have it on tape. To her frustration, Jason merely nodded.

She tried another angle of attack. "How did Kevin find out about it?"

"It was my damn assistant, Sheila! She noticed a discrepancy in one of the financial reports that came through my office. She dug further into it and then told Kevin what she had found." He snorted out a laugh. "Of course, the jerk figured out a way to use the information to make money. I wanted to fire her, but they had me over a barrel. I got her in the end though, It was Sheila who delivered the fatal cupcakes to Kevin!" He gave a full out laugh which ended in a high pitched, hysterical note.

Great, he's delusional and deranged.

"Jason, why did you use my cupcakes to poison him? Surely you could have found some other food to put it in."

"Ah...*that* was the brilliant part of my plan. With the history between the two of you, I knew poisoning him with your cupcakes would throw them off *my* track while they investigated *you*. Plus, it was a little insurance policy to make sure you would go away with me." He eyed her up and down. "Just in case you resisted, I knew you wouldn't want to stay here and face jail time."

Lexy could only shake her head at his faulty logic. The man clearly needed dating advice if he thought setting her up for murder was a way to make her want to run away with him.

Jason continued on, unaware that Lexy was edging her way towards the door. “Kevin was so cocky, so sure of himself. Threatening to turn me in. I mean I’m his brother for crying out lout!”

“Turn you in with the information in the book?” Lexy asked, still holding it.

“Yes, of course.” Jason’s eyes narrowed to slits. “Wait a minute - let me see what’s in there.”

Lexy tried to pull the book out of his reach, but he was too fast, grabbing it roughly out of her hands. He opened the book. Her heart clenched in terror. Lexy could see his face growing redder as he realized he’d been duped.

‘You bitch!” He screamed. “You tricked me - just like Kevin!”

Lexy’s brain was screaming for her to run but her legs felt like tree trunks rooted to the spot. Jason’s eyes were wild, his face a mask of rage.

"No one crosses me," he sputtered. "You saw what happened to Kevin when he tried it - he got his and now you'll get yours too!

Jason lunged for Lexy, wrapping his hands around her throat. Squeezing with all his might. Lexy tried to fend him off, but her air supply was dwindling, stars swam before her eyes. Everything was starting to turn black. She thought of Nans and Sprinkles. *What would they do without her?*

Jason's face, only inches from hers, was screwed up in anger as he focused his energy on choking the life out of her. With one last burst of strength, she reached into her purse. Her hand closed on a round cylinder. She brought her hand up in between their faces, pressed the button on the cylinder and sprayed.

Lexy heard Jason scream, then felt him release his hold on her neck. She slumped to the floor gasping for air but finding only the heavy mist of pepper spray which her lungs violently coughed out again.

Hearing a thunderous crash and the sound of splintering wood, she peered through teary eyes towards the direction of the sound just in time to see Jack and several members of the BRPD come barreling through the door with their guns drawn.

Chapter Sixteen

Lexy was sputtering and coughing, her eyes watering from the pepper spray. She felt strong arms wrap around her, pulling her to her feet.

"Lexy, are you OK?" Jack's face was etched with lines of concern.

"I ... think ... so." She managed to get the words out between coughs. On the other side of the room, she saw Jason face down on the floor with two detectives trying to wrestle him into handcuffs. His violent yelling and squirming wasn't making the job easy for them.

"What were you thinking?" Jack demanded. "You could have been killed!"

Lexy felt her cheeks grow hot, she looked down at the floor. She *had* been foolish to confront Jason herself. She had been thinking of him as her old friend and had forgotten how dangerous he was.

Jack tilted her chin up with his thumb, forcing her to look at him. He wiped a tear from her cheek. The tender look in his eyes made her heart melt.

Then his lips were on hers causing her body to tingle. Her stomach did a little flip flop. She leaned in, accepting his kiss. She forgot about everything, losing herself in the delicious sensations that were rippling through her. Then, she remembered he had a *girlfriend*.

She pulled away like a child pulling their hand back from a hot stove. Jack's eyes flew open, a startled look on his face.

"Is something wrong?"

"You know what's wrong. You shouldn't be kissing me like that! What would your girlfriend think?" Lexy felt hot, searing anger replacing the warm tingly feelings that had been there just a moment ago.

'Girlfriend? What are you talking about?"

"Don't try to deny it! I heard you calling her *darling* on the phone and saw her in your livin room window one night with her long, curly hair!" Lexy was close to tears. *Why did she feel so hurt?*

Jack stared at her for a moment, his forehead wrinkled in confusion. Then she saw the wrinkles disappear. He let out a deep, long laugh.

"You think that was my *girlfriend*?" His eyes twinkled with amusement. He turned, poking his head out the door. "Hey John, come in here for a minute."

Lexy stood there bristling with anger. *Just what did he think was so funny?* Lexy glanced over seeing a man saunter through the door. Black leather jacket, torn jeans, hair slicked back in a pony tail. *An undercover detective?*

"This is my partner, John *Darling*." Jack said with emphasis on the detectives last name.

"He usually wears his hair all loose and curly, but today he has the pony tail." John turned around to show off his lengthy locks. "I'm guessing *he's* the one you saw at my house."

Lexy felt her jaw drop open. Even though she felt like a fool, she couldn't help but see the humor in it. She held her hand out to the detective.

"Nice to meet you," she said, stifling a giggle.

He took her hand, shaking it firmly. "So you're the one who's caused all the ruckus downtown?" He said with a wink.

"I am?"

"Sure, Jack's been working overtime all week trying to get you crossed off the suspect list so you can reopen your bakery..."

He was interrupted by a commotion on their right. The other detectives were hauling Jason past them towards the door. He wasn't going easily.

"There's my cue to leave." John said. He joined the others, helping them push the soon to be former deputy mayor out the door to the waiting police car.

Jack turned to Lexy, tucking a stray hair behind her ear.

"Lexy, I don't have a girlfriend," he said. "I'm not the kind of guy who does that sort of thing... I'm not like Kevin.

Lexy nodded. “I’m sorry, I guess I jumped to conclusions.”

“Well, now *that’s* cleared up, I think we might have some unfinished business...” Jack leaned down towards her. Lexy eagerly stood on her tip toes to meet him. This time she didn’t worry about girlfriends, murderers or cheating boyfriends as she surrendered herself fully to his spine tingling, toe curling kiss.

Epilogue

"I still don't understand how you figured out it was Jason." Cassie was boxing up the umpteenth package of cupcake tops they had sold that morning.

Lexy looked around the bakery - it was packed full of customers. All her worries about the bakery being closed and the negative publicity hurting business had been for nothing. Quite the opposite had happened. The notoriety of her "Killer Cupcakes" had increased business. Everyone wanted to try a taste of her infamous cupcake tops.

"After I got knocked out, Sprinkles found a button on the floor. It wasn't one of mine, so I figured it must be from whoever knocked me out. Then I saw Jason on TV at Nans and recognized the button on his jacket. I remembered Jason had worn a strange pine scented aftershave at Kevin's wake - I had smelled the same smell when I was on the floor after being knocked out. I put two and two together and knew it was him!" Lexy smiled with pride at her skills of deduction.

"And you decided to confront him yourself? Seems pretty dangerous - you should have at least called me ... or Jack. Speak of the devil." Cassie nodded her chin over towards the bakery door.

Lexy looked over at Jack standing in the doorway. Her heart did a little flip. She ran over to greet him, taking his hand, she pulled him to one of the tables. Grabbing a couple of coffee's from her self serve station, she took a seat across the table from him and pushed one of the coffees at him.

"I had a visit from a strange man yesterday at the station," Jack said, fixing his honey brown eyes on her.

"Oh?" Lexy tilted her head raising an eyebrow.

"He said he was a friend of Kevin's and had talked to you at the wake."

Lexy remembered the disheveled man who had threatened her. "I think I know who you mean - I told you about him, didn't I?"

Jack nodded. "He said he knew all about the whole blackmail scheme - although he claims he was not involved. Anyway, he said Kevin was afraid something might happen to him. Kevin sent you the book because he knew he could trust you. I think he meant to talk to you about it but was killed before he could. The man said he was just trying to warn you so you wouldn't get hurt."

"Oh well that's a relief." Lexy settled back in her chair. "So, the case is all wrapped up now?"

"Pretty much... we still need to find Sheila. She seems to have disappeared along with the blackmai money Kevin had collected."

Lexy took a long sip of her coffee, letting the bitter sweet liquid swirl around her taste buds. I Kevin had treated Sheila the way he treated her then the girl deserved to get away with the money.

Jack reached across the table, putting his hand over Lexy's. "Are we still on for tonight?"

Lexy's stomach did summersaults at the way h looked at her. It had only been a couple of day since they had arrested Jason but Lexy and Jack ha already been on one, wonderful date. She couldn't wait for more.

Lexy nodded enthusiastically. Jack's eyes gazed into hers, his thumb caressed her palm causing chills to run up her spine. *How did he expect her to keep her mind on work all day?*

The tingle of the bell over the door broke the moment. Lexy looked over to see John Darling's long legged frame in the doorway. Out of the corner of her eye, she saw Cassie give him the once over. Lexy giggled to herself - John was exactly Cassie's type.

John's eyes scanned the room, lingering for a moment on Cassie, then settling on Jack and Lexy. "We gotta go." He said to Jack, then nodded a greeting at Lexy.

Jack jumped up. "I'll see you around seven?" He said, looking pointedly at her.

Lexy nodded giving a little wave. Jack turned following John out the door. Just as the door shut, she saw John turn around and give Cassie a second look over his shoulder. She glanced over at Cassie who was standing behind the counter, her mouth hanging open.

"Who was *that*?" She asked, wide eyed.

"Oh, he's Jacks partner - John Darling." Lexy said with a smile.

"Phew." Cassie fanned herself with her hand. "The BRPD sure has some fine police detectives. Maybe we should get mixed up in more murder cases."

Lexy laughed. She had to admit tracking down Kevin's killer had been an interesting challenge. She enjoyed putting together the clues and the rush of that final moment when all the pieces fell into place and she figured out who it was. But tracking down murderers was a lot of work and very time consuming. She'd rather spend all her time here at the bakery, doing what she loved - baking.

Besides, tracking down *one* killer was enough for an entire lifetime - wasn't it?

The End.

Ready For More? Get The Rest Of The Lexy Baker Series Today at

http://www.leighanndobbs.com:

Dying For Danish (Lexy Baker Bakery Series Book 2) - When Lexy Baker lands a high paying catering job that allows her to buy some much needed kitchen equipment, she's excited that things are going so well ... until she stumbles over the body of the bride-to-be.

Suddenly Lexy finds herself in a race against time to find the killer. Aided by four iPad toting amateur detective grandma's, her best friend and her little dog Sprinkles, Lexy finds the suspect list growing at every turn.

To make matters worse, the investigation is headed up by her hunky neighbor Detective Jack Perillo who she had been hot and heavy with - until he mysteriously stopped calling her several weeks earlier.

Add a handsome, rich bachelor who is also a suspect and seems to have designs on Lexy to the mix, and Lexy soon finds that things are not what they seem.

Will Lexy be able to catch the killer in time, or will she end up Dying for Danish?

Murder, Money and Marzipan (Lexy Baker Bakery Series Book 3) - When Lexy Baker makes it to the finale of America's most prestigious bakery contest, Bakery Battles, she thinks her biggest dream has finally come true...

Until she stumbles across the dead body of judge Amanda Scott-Saunders.

What starts out as a bad day for Lexy becomes even worse when the police discover the judge was strangled with Lexy's apron. Now Lexy's sitting at the top of the suspect list with a motive, means and opportunity... but no solid alibi.

Lexy soon finds herself in a race against time to find the real killer before she ends up disqualified from the contest, or worse, in jail. But that's no easy task. There's a bakery competition full of suspects who all hated the victim and have a $100,000 motive for murder. And then there's the gorgeous, smart police detective who has mysterious ties to Lexy's boyfriend and thinks Lexy is the killer.

Luckily Lexy has a secret weapon -- her iPad-toting grandmother. As long as Lexy can lure Nans away from the slot machines, she and her gang of senior citizen amateur detectives can help Lexy sift through the clues to uncover the startling truth about the real killer.

With a $100,000 grand prize at stake and the search for the killer heating up -- will Lexy clear her name in time to grab the prize... or will her dream turn into a nightmare?

3 Bodies and a Biscotti ***(Lexy Baker Bakery Series Book 4)*** **-** There's a serial killer on the loose. And Lexy Baker's grandmother, Nans, could be the next victim.

The bodies are piling up at the Brook Ridge Falls Retirement Center. Healthy people are dropping like flies. And yet no one believes a murderer is on the loose... except for Lexy Baker and the troupe of iPad-toting grandmothers who live at the center.

When Lexy's detective boyfriend, Jack, refuses to believe that foul play is involved, Lexy has no choice but to find the killer on her own. Along with Nans and her gang of iPad-toting, mystery-solving grandmas, they use everything from hypnosis to high-tech gadgets to track down the killer.

Meanwhile, Jack is acting strange. People are snickering mysteriously behind Lexy's back. And Lexy discovers eating all those sweets is finally catching up with her. Soon she finds herself in a race against time as she juggles dropping a few pounds, preparing for a surprise wedding, patching up her relationship with Jack, and finding the killer.

Will Lexy uncover the killer's shocking identity before their next victim dies?

Recipe

Lexy's Famous Cupcake Tops

Everyone knows that the best part of the cupcake is the top with all that delicious frosting. That's why it's no secret that cupcake tops are a favorite at Lexy's bakery - *The Cup and Cake.* Here's how to make them in your own kitchen:

Ingredients:

1 1/3 cups flour

3/4 cup unsweetened cocoa powder

2 teaspoons baking powder

1/4 teas baking soda

1/8 tsp salt

1 1/2 cups sugar

3 tbsp butter, softened

2 eggs

1 tsp vanilla

1/2 cup strong brewed coffee (Lexy likes to use espresso)

1/2 cup milk

Preparation:

Preheat oven to 350 F (175C).

In a medium bowl, sift the flour, cocoa powder, baking powder and baking soda together.

In a large bowl, cream the butter and sugar until fluffy. Add the eggs one by one, beating well after each. Add vanilla.

Add the flour mixture to the sugar mixture, mix well and then add the coffee and milk. Beat well.

Spoon the batter into muffin cups taking care to only fill them 3/4 of the way full.

Bake for 15 minutes or until a toothpick comes out clean.

Let the cupcakes cool.

Cut off the cupcake tops, right where they meet the cupcake liners. You can do this with a long knife, or, take some dental floss - pull it tight between your hands and run it under the cupcake tops.

Once you have the tops off, you can frost them - I've provided Lexy's favorite frosting recipe below.

Lexy's Favorite Frosting Recipe

Ingredients:

2 sticks butter, softened

3 1/2 cups confectioners sugar

1 teaspoon heavy cream

1 teaspoon vanilla bean paste

1/8 tsp salt

Preparation:

Cream the butter, sugar and salt together.

Mix the cream and vanilla paste together and add a little at a time until you get the desired consistency. If you don't have vanilla bean paste you can substitute 1 teaspoon vanilla extract.

Things You Can Do With The Cupcake Bottoms

Now you might be wondering what to do with the cupcake bottoms. You don't want to waste them! Lexy uses them to make truffle - just pile them into a truffle bowl along with pudding and whipped cream for a delicious dessert.

You could also use them as little mini cakes, or cut them up into different shapes with cookie cutters and make them into little desserts or build sculpted cakes out of them. Use your imagination, but whatever you do, don't let them go to waste!

About the Author

Leighann Dobbs lives in New Hampshire with her husband and their trusty Chihuahua mix Mojo and beautiful rescue cat, Kitty. She likes to write romance short stories and novelettes perfect for the busy person on the go. These stories are great for someone who doesn't have a lot of time for reading a full novel. Why not pick one up and escape to another time and place the next time you are waiting for an appointment, enjoying a bath or waiting to pick up the kids at soccer?

Find out about her latest books and how to get her next book for free by signing up at:

http://www.leighanndobbs.com

Connect with Leighann on Facebook and Twitter

http://facebook.com/leighanndobbsbooks

http://twitter.com/leighanndobbs

About the Author

Made in the USA
Monee, IL
06 July 2021

73017906R00085